WILD WEST

A TIME TRAVEL ADVENTURE

VICTORIA RUSH

VOLUME 2

RILEY'S TIME TRAVEL ADVENTURES - BOOK 2

COPYRIGHT

For the uninhibited...

WANT TO AMP UP YOUR SEX LIFE?

Sign up for my newsletter to receive more free books and other steamy stuff. Discover a hundred different ways to wet your whistle!

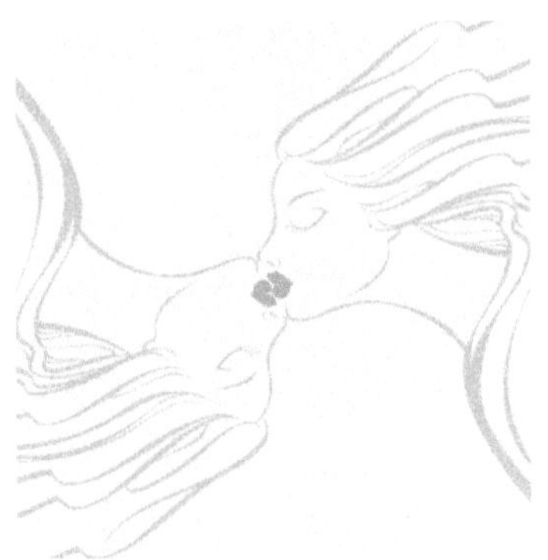

Victoria Rush Erotica

1

After her exciting time travel adventure to the 18th century Caribbean, Riley was eager to see where her intriguing machine would take her next. She still had no idea how it worked, or even if it would start up again, but when she pressed the on button on the side, the smartphone screen suddenly lit up, displaying the familiar image of the swirling funnel. As it began to shake violently in her hand, the funnel began rising above the glass surface. She could feel the power of the vortex pulling her toward it, and she reached out to touch her friend's cheek before raising her other hand up to the edge of the cloud.

Suddenly, she felt herself pulled into the cyclone and tumbling through the three-dimensional portal, unsure where or when she would land. After a few minutes, she dropped onto a rickety bed in a small wood-framed room overlooking the main street of a dusty frontier town. Not long after, a man wearing a cowboy hat and a pair of Colt revolvers on his belt entered the room, closing the door behind him. When he saw Riley's naked body lying on top of the sheets, he smiled and unbuckled his belt, advancing toward the shaking schoolgirl.

"I haven't seen *you* around here before," he smirked, stepping out of his cowboy boots and unstrapping his chaps. "But you'll do just fine satisfying my appetite–"

"What? No..." Riley said, standing up to defend herself against the man's advance. "I don't know who you think I am, but I'm not going to have sex with you."

"No?" the man sneered. "You work in a brothel and you don't want to have sex with me? We'll see about that."

As he moved closer toward Riley with his dick swinging at half-mast between his legs, she waited until he was within striking distance, then she kicked him as hard as she could with a snap-kick to his balls. The man doubled over in agony, grasping his scrotum, then he reached behind him for his pistol, turning around to point it toward Riley. She glanced around, looking for something to defend herself, noticing a broom in the corner. When she picked it up and swung the handle toward the man, he paused for a moment, laughing menacingly.

"You've got spunk, I'll give you that," he sniggered. "I'm going to enjoy taming you."

As he advanced slowly toward her, Riley braced her feet the way Liza had taught her when they practiced sword fighting, then she swung the handle rapidly downward, striking the man on his right wrist. His pistol tilted toward the floor, firing a loud round into the floorboards, and he reared up, preparing to strike her with his fist. She lunged forward, driving the tip of the broom into his solar plexus, then she struck him as hard as she could on the side of his temple.

When he crumpled unconscious onto the floor, an attractive middle-aged woman wearing a push-up corset swung open the door, peering at the naked girl and the man lying on the floor with his bare ass pointing upward.

"Who the hell are you?" she said. "And what have you done to my best customer?"

"U m..." Riley stammered, unsure how to explain her mysterious circumstances. "My name's Riley and this man was trying to rape me."

The woman peered at Riley with a blank expression, then glanced downward at the prostrated man on the floor.

"You *do* realize this is a brothel?" she said. "And that this man was simply partaking in what call girls are expected to provide?"

"I'm not a call girl," Riley said.

"Then what the hell are you doing buck naked in one of my private rooms?"

Riley stared at the woman for a moment, realizing she'd never believe her far-fetched story of traveling through time from a different era.

"To be honest, I'm not exactly sure how I landed here. It's all a bit of a blur, really..."

"Well, this wouldn't be the first time a drunken patron found themselves led upstairs unawares," the woman chuckled, looking around the room. "Where are your clothes?"

"I guess they got lost somewhere in the shuffle," Riley said, picking up one of the bed pillows to cover her bare midriff, noticing the edge of her smartphone sticking out from the side of the other pillow.

Suddenly, the man on the floor groaned, rubbing the side of his bruised head. The woman helped him to his feet, and when he recognized Riley, he stepped toward her threateningly. The woman grabbed his arm, moving between him and the schoolgirl.

"Whoa there, Amos. This girl doesn't actually work here. There's plenty of other saloon girls that can look after your needs if you're still feeling in the mood."

The man glared at Riley for a moment, then bent down to pull up his clothes.

"She has a funny way of showing it," he said, running his eyes up and down the girl's partly covered body. "This won't be the last time the two of us have words. Next time, try locking the door if you don't want any extra company."

After the man exited the room, the woman closed the door behind him, latching it shut with an old key.

"You seem plenty sobered up now," she said, turning back toward Riley. "Where is your home?"

"Somewhere pretty far away," Riley shrugged. "I was just passing through..."

The woman walked over to a chest of drawers lining the opposite wall and pulled out some fresh clothes.

"Well, we can't have you prancing around naked and distracting all my customers if you're not going to service their needs. You can wear these for now."

She held up a corset, petticoat, and camisole for Riley to put on, then placed the items on the end of the bed.

"Thank you," Riley said, glancing at the old-fashioned garments. "But I'm not sure I'll be able to find my way back home. May I stay here until I find my bearings?"

"I suppose so," the woman nodded. "But you'll have to earn your keep like all the other girls."

"You mean as a–"

"We can probably find something for you to do *down-stairs* if you prefer. Do you think you'll be able to manage your temper if I set you up as a barmaid?"

"You mean serving food and beverages to your customers?" Riley said. "That sounds easy enough."

"You'll have to share a room with one of the other girls," the woman said. "Room and board will be provided as long as you prove yourself useful. Get yourself cleaned up, then meet me downstairs, where I'll introduce you to the kitchen staff."

The woman placed her key in the lock and opened the door, preparing to exit the room.

"Wait!" Riley said, calling out to her. "I don't even know your name."

"You can call me Madame, like the rest of the girls and customers."

"Yes Ma'am," Riley said as the woman closed the door softly behind her.

Then she shook her head, peering down at the Victorian-era undergarments lying at the foot of the bed.

Next time, remember to put on some clothes before turning on the phone, she murmured to herself before placing the time travel device above the window valence, where no one would find it.

2

———

Riley picked up the strange vestments lying on the bed, unsure what to put on first. She rolled the fabric of the knee-length stockings between her fingers, nodding approvingly.

Silk, she said to herself. *Thank heavens they haven't invented nylon yet.*

She pulled the stockings on, fastening the garters above her knees, then pulled the baggy bloomers over her hips, squinting at the large buttoned flap at the front.

It's a far cry from Victoria's Secret, she chuckled, stepped in front of the dressing mirror next to the armoire to look at herself. *But at least they're comfortable enough.*

Then she picked up the V-shaped corset, wrapping it around her waist. It had metal clasps on the front, and she had to suck in her stomach to close the two sides. When she looked in the mirror, her waist was tightly cinched, with the top of her breasts spilling over the top of the bodice.

Jesus, she said. *How do women breathe in this thing? So much for wearing comfortable clothes.*

The next item was a ruffled petticoat with a wire cage at

the back to make it flare over the hips. She pulled it up over her bloomers and tied it around her waist, then turned sideways to peer at the strange shape of her derriere formed by the contraption.

Eat your heart out, Jennifer Lopez, Riley laughed, looking at the flared bustle. *At least I won't have to go to the gym to keep my ass firm and round.*

When she wrapped the knee-length embroidered skirt around her waist and clasped it in the front, she noticed the lower edge rested a few inches above the ruffled hem of the petticoat.

A bit of a tease, she nodded, turning her body from side to side, admiring her hourglass profile and plump breasts.

The last item to put on was a lacy camisole that barely covered her corset. After she buttoned up the front, she glanced at the full ensemble in the mirror, nodding softly.

It's funny the ways women highlighted their female assets in different eras, she thought. The wire bustle and push-up corset were the opposite of the modern-day aesthetic of skinny jeans and plunging cleavages. But she rather liked the look, even though it felt strange to sit on the edge of the bed with the wire cage pressing in to the side of her waist as she stooped down to put on the patent leather pumps.

When she stepped out of her room and headed down the hall toward the stairs leading downstairs, some of the passing brothel customers peered at her, wondering who the new girl was. As she descended the stairs toward the noisy saloon, all eyes seemed to follow her while she tried not to trip over her bulky train and high heels.

She noticed the madame standing at the edge of the bar talking to a customer wearing a black cowboy hat, and when she approached the couple, she smiled.

"That looks a little more presentable," she nodded. "Did everything fit alright?"

"I don't know how you manage to breathe in this outfit all day long," Riley chuckled, adjusting her tight-fitting corset with two hands. "Not to mention go to the bathroom with all these layers on."

"I don't know where *you* come from," Madame said. "But this is how women dress in these parts."

"Are you going to introduce me to the new girl?" the man in the black hat said.

Riley peered at his leather vest, noticing a silver star on his chest.

"Of course," Madame said. "Riley, this is our town sheriff, James Mason. James, this is my new barmaid, Riley."

"Pleased to meet you, Riley," the sheriff said, extending his hand as he peered down at her puffy breasts. "Though I must say I'm disappointed to hear you'll only be working *downstairs*."

"Um, yes," Riley said, unsure how to respond to his thinly veiled pass. "Technically, I haven't started working yet."

"Well, it appears that I'm not the *only* one looking forward to your getting started," he said, peering around the room at the patrons ogling the comely newcomer.

"Let's get you introduced to the rest of the staff," Madame said, intertwining her arm around Riley's. "I'll be seeing you around, James."

"I'm sure you will," the sheriff said, stealing another glance at Riley's cleavage before he ambled off to chat with some of the other saloon patrons.

"Is everybody here so–*direct* in their comportment?" Riley said, her heaving bosom belying her elevated heart rate.

"They don't call it the Wild West for nothing," Madame nodded. "You just have to learn to let these sorts of affronts slide over you. Otherwise, you'll get yourself into more trouble than it's worth."

"I'm not sure I'm properly equipped to protect myself against any more trouble," Riley said, noticing every saloon customer wearing a belt with a gun on his hips.

"Where did you say you were from again?" Madame said. "Have you ever fired a gun before?"

"I didn't, but I'm originally from Boston. People don't exactly carry their guns out in the open back there."

"Boston?" the Madame said, raising her eyebrows. "You're a long way from home. You need to know how to defend herself in these parts. I'll take you out to my ranch sometime for some target practice. You *do* know how to ride a horse?"

"Um..."

"Oh my God," Madame sighed. "You really *are* a big city girl. Let's hope you know how to balance a food platter."

"I think I can manage that much," Riley laughed.

"This is Clarence, our bartender," Madame said, tilting her head toward the tall, heavy-set man behind the counter sporting a handlebar moustache. "He'll be supplying you with most of you customer orders. People come here to drink more often than stuff their gullets."

"Among other things," Clarence chuckled.

"Let's take a tour of the kitchen," Madame said, motioning for Riley to follow her down a hall leading to the rear of the saloon.

"These are the restrooms," she said, pointing out a line of unisex cubicles lining the wall. "Though you might want to use the outhouse behind the kitchen. The customer lavatories can get a little messy by the end of the day, what with all the drunken card players and all."

After Madame introduced Riley to the cook and the rest of the saloon girls, she handed her a small notepad and a pencil.

"If you're ready to get started, I've assigned you tables one through five. You'll see the numbers etched in the glass lamps above each table. All you have to do is take the customer orders, then pass them along to Henry or Clarence, who'll place your completed orders on the serving counter."

"Sounds simple enough," Riley nodded, peering up at the price list scrawled on a blackboard above the bar. "Where will I deposit the receipts?"

"Pass your earnings together with a copy of the bill to Clarence, who'll store it in the cash register. Some of the patrons have a nasty habit of wandering hands. If you're not careful, you can easily be pilfered off your takings."

Riley dug her hands into the pockets of her skirt, making a note to keep a mindful eye as she circulated among the tables.

"Right," she said. "Watch out for wandering hands."

When Madame took her leave to mingle among the patrons, Riley strolled over to her assigned section of the room, noticing her wide skirt and bustle brushing against the sides of the narrowly spaced tables and chairs. When she stopped at one of the tables filled with a group of boisterous card players, they peered up at her with an amused expression.

"Would you like something to eat or drink?" she said, trying to still her racing heart.

"Why yes," one of the cowboys said. "I think we would. What do you say boys, are you hungry for some fresh meat?"

"Don't say if I do," another player said, tilting his head up and down as he appraised Riley's fulsome figure. "Are *you* on the menu as well?"

"I'm afraid not," Riley said. "I only work the downstairs room."

"Pity," the man said. "Because you look awfully tender and juicy."

"You're new here," the first cowboy smiled. "Where are you from, darling?"

"Back east," Riley said, thinking it best not to reveal any unnecessary details to the rowdy pack.

"I thought I detected a New England accent," he said. "How long will you be staying with us?"

"I'm not sure," Riley said. "I was just passing through. Thought I'd get the lay of the land before deciding on my next destination."

"Well, you just let us know if you need any help with that," the cowboy said, winking at his friends around the table. "That is, with getting the lay of the land."

"Did you wish to place an order?" Riley said, ignoring the cowboy's suggestive comments. "I've got other tables I need to attend to."

"Why don't you just top us up with four more ales?" the man said. "But keep an eye on our glasses. The beer in this place isn't much stronger than watered-down piss."

"I'll be back in a moment," Riley said, scribbling the order and table number on her notepad.

As she turned to head back toward the bar, one of the cowboys reached out to pinch the side of her buttocks, and Riley flinched. Thinking discretion the better part of valor on her first working day, she ignored the affront, picking up the order at the front counter and returning to place each of the steins on the table beside the cowboys. As she leaned over to place the mugs, the men rubbed their shoulders against her dress, turning their faces within inches of her bulging bosom.

With each return to the table to top up their glasses, the increasingly intoxicated players became bolder in their touching and leering, tickling her breeches and blowing on her exposed cleavage. It took everything in her power not to slap them, and by the time she returned to the counter to pick up another order, her cheeks were flushed with rage.

"How's it going over there?" one of the bargirls said, noticing the sweat on Riley's brow.

"It's a little more touchy-feely than I expected," Riley sighed, slamming the refilled glasses down on her serving platter.

"You get used to it after a while," the girl said. "If they get too indiscreet, just stop serving them. They'll get the message sooner or later. If things get out of hand, ask Clarence to escort them out of the establishment. It won't be the first time he's had to boot someone out of here for inappropriate behavior."

"Thanks," Riley said, extending her hand. "I'm Riley, what's your name?"

"Bess," the girl said, clasping Riley's hand. "I think Madame has us rooming together. Perhaps I can give you some tips later on for dealing with these miscreants."

"I'll look forward to that," Riley said, noticing the girl's billowing bosom while she peered back at her. "Any quick advice before I go back into the lion's den?"

"Just don't take any shit," Bess said. "If you give these guys an inch, they'll take a mile."

"Right," Riley said, picking up her platter and carrying a new round of drinks back to the table.

This time, when she leaned over to place one of the glasses on the table next to one of the players, he reached under her skirt, sliding his fingers up the inside of her thighs. Without hesitating, she picked up his full glass, throwing the contents into his face. The man paused for a moment in shock, then he stood up, grabbing Riley around the neck with one hand.

"Who the hell do you think you are, *trollop*?" he hollered, shaking Riley violently as she stood on her tiptoes.

She tried to kick the man, but her thick petticoat and bustle prevented her from gaining any traction, and as her face reddened from lack of breath, she peered out of the corner of her eye, noticing a hulking man approaching the table.

"You'll take your hands off the lady if you know what's good for you, Charlie," Clarence said, pointing a shotgun at his head.

The man peered at Clarence for a moment, then he dropped his hand from Riley's neck, smiling nervously.

"It was just a little misunderstanding is all," the cowboy said, moving his hand closer to his revolver.

"Yeah, well, you can clear your head outside until you sober up. And that goes for the *rest* of you, if there are any other misunderstandings today."

"No worries," the ringleader said, motioning for the rest of his crew to leave the establishment, dropping a few coins on the table. "We'll have to stop our game anyhow, without a full hand. Sorry for the trouble, m'lady."

As the posse stumbled out of the saloon together, Madame came over to inspect Riley's neck, lifting her chin gently.

"I think you've had enough work for your first day," she said, leading Riley over to the base of the stairs. "Let's get you cleaned up and rested. It appears that I neglected to give you adequate training for this job."

As Riley limped toward the stairs, she noticed the sheriff standing in the corner with a few other men, smirking at her while the two women headed upstairs. She pinched her eyebrows, wondering why he hadn't bothered to intercede and take the troublemaker into custody.

But it didn't matter. Just like on the pirate ship, she knew she'd have to learn some new methods of self-defense in this new, wild frontier.

3

———

After Madame took Riley upstairs and tended to her sore neck, she lay her to rest in one of the private rooms, locking the door softly behind her. Riley soon fell asleep, exhausted from all the excitement of the day, and when she awoke a few hours later, she heard a key tinkling in the lock. Sitting up concerned it might be another interloper, she pulled the bedsheets over her naked body, staring at the door with a racing pulse. When she saw that it was the saloon girl, Bess, she slumped back against her pillow, relieved.

"Were you able to sleep after all that commotion earlier in the day?" Bess said, closing the door behind her.

"Yes," Riley nodded, letting the sheets slide over her breasts. "It's been a long day in more ways than one."

"Well, you can relax for the rest of the evening," Bess said. "Our work is done for the day. Now it's the *other* working girls' turn to entertain our customers."

"That's a relief," Riley said, suddenly feeling the need to relieve herself. "But I'm not looking forward to having to put on all of those layers of clothes just to go downstairs to pee."

Bess walked over to the armoire and removed a long linen chemise from the compartment.

"You can put this on for now," she said. "Use the back stairs to avoid the saloon customers. There's an outhouse in the back."

Riley scampered out of bed and after donning the chemise, she tiptoed down the hall past the noisy main hall and out the back door, past the tumbleweed to the creaky outhouse set back a few hundred feet from the main building. When she opened the door, she recoiled at the smell of the interior, glancing at the round hole carved out of the soiled wooden bench. Holding her nose, she pulled up her chemise and tensed her leg muscles, trying not to touch the filthy commode with any part of her body.

She found it odd that there was no toilet paper or sink in the lavatory, and when she finished her business, she flung open the door to escape the noxious fumes, rattling a string of corn cobs dangling beside the entrance. Eager to get back to the relative safety and comfort of her private quarters, she hurried up the back stairs, closing the door quickly behind her.

"Everything okay?" Bess said, beginning to undress. "You look like you've just seen a ghost."

"I wish I had," Riley panted. "At least that might have kept me distracted from the foul smell of the outhouse."

"We have to go *somewhere*," Bess said. "At least you have a degree of privacy out back."

"Doesn't anybody stock toilet paper in there?"

"Toilet paper?"

"You know, for cleaning your behind."

"Maybe that's what they use in your fancy parlors back East, but out *here*, we use corn husks or mullein leaves to wipe our asses."

"How quaint," Riley said, shaking her head in dismay. "What about running water? How do you clean the rest of your body after sitting on that filthy bench?"

"There's not much plumbing out here in Wild West," Bess said, motioning to the cast iron bathtub resting in the corner of the room. "We use chamber pots and baths to clean up when necessary. Would you like me to fill the tub with warm water?"

"That would be heavenly," Riley said, eager to get the stench of stale beer and soot off her body.

Bess walked over to a chain hanging next to the window, and when she pulled it, a soft bell sounded. A few minutes later, there was a knock on the door and when she opened it, a stout Asian man stood in the doorway, balancing two heavy pails of steaming water on a yoke over his neck. Bess motioned for him to empty the water into the bathtub, and when he turned to leave, she handed him two copper coins.

"That's *one* way to get your water delivered," Riley chuckled after the man shut the door.

"We don't have a lot of luxuries out here in Cody, but Joon looks after us pretty well."

Bess peered at the tub, removing her clothing.

"Shall we?"

"Were you planning on *joining* me?" Riley said, peering at the girl's hourglass figure and firm breasts.

"Why not?" Bess said. "There's enough room for both of us. I need to soothe my sore feet too."

The two women dipped their toes in the warm water and as they slid their naked bodies down the opposite sides of the slanted basin, their asses pressed together while they intertwined their legs beside one another's chest and shoulders.

"Does that feel better?" Bess said, rocking her hips gently against Riley's.

"Much," Riley sighed, feeling Bess's pussy rubbing up against hers under the steaming water.

"Madame says you're from Boston," Bess said, beginning to massage Riley's feet resting next to her breasts.

"In a roundabout way," Riley nodded.

"You seem a little out of your element in these parts," Bess said, smiling at Riley as she worked her hands up her legs. "Whatever inspired you to come all this way?"

"It's a long story," Riley said. "Let's just say it wasn't by choice."

"Oh," Bess grinned, pressing her thumbs into Riley's calf muscles. "The mystery deepens. That's okay–most of the girls in this saloon have a past they'd rather forget also."

"What about you?" Riley said, lifting one of Bess's legs to return the favor. "How did you end up here?"

"My husband died over an unfortunate dispute. The madame was kind enough to offer me a job at the saloon when we lost our ranch."

"Dispute?" Riley said. "What *kind* of dispute?"

"It was a misunderstanding over a card game. One of the players accused my husband of stealing and challenged him to a duel."

"There seems to be a lot of that going around," Riley nodded. "What kind of a duel?"

"A gun battle in the main street. Everybody came out to watch."

"Is that how people settle their disputes around here?" Riley said, pausing her massage of Bess's leg just below her knee.

"Most of them," Bess said. "The gun rules the day in the wild frontier, and the quickest man is the last one alive."

"Madame thinks I should learn how to shoot a gun too," Riley said, massaging Bess's calves.

"It can't hurt," Bess cooed, sliding down deeper under the water to press her hips harder against Riley's ass. "You never know when you might need to defend yourself with this wild and unscrupulous lot."

"Do you miss your husband?" Riley said, rocking her ass softly against Bess.

"Sometimes on lonely nights," she smiled, rolling her wet fingers further up the inside of Riley's thigh. "But there's plenty of other people around here to satisfy my needs."

"Oh?" Riley grinned. "Do you do a little side business with the customers from time to time?"

"It's hard enough trying to fend off the horny cowboys as it is," Bess said, shaking her head. "If they know you're available for a quick roll in the private rooms, they'll never keep their hands off you."

"You don't like hands on you?" Riley smiled, leaning closer toward Bess as she slid her fingers up her warm thigh.

"Not *theirs*," Bess said, pulling her face to within a few inches of Riley's. "I prefer the soft fingers of you New England doves."

"Mmm," Riley purred, mashing her breasts against Bess's as she slid her tongue into her mouth.

Some things never change wherever my time machine takes me, she thought. *No matter where I go, people always need intimacy and the touch of a tender body...*

4

———

After Riley and Bess made love in the bathtub, they both slept soundly together in the lone double bed until Madame entered the room shortly before noon.

"Wake up, sleepy-heads," she said, walking over to the window and pulling open the drapes.

Noticing the tub still filled with water, she pulled up the lower pane then scooped out the liquid with a metal pail in the corner, tossing it out the window.

"Time to get to work," she said. "The bar's already starting to fill up with hungry cowboys."

"Ugh," Bess groaned, shuffling out of bed to put on her bloomers. "Sometimes I wish we weren't the only saloon in town. It would be nice to have a day off once in a while."

"At least *one* of you will," Madame smiled. "I'll be taking Riley out to my ranch today for a little target practice. She'll need to develop a tougher skin if she's going to survive out here in the wild frontier."

"Well don't toughen her up *too* much," Bess said,

glancing at Riley's lithe figure as she pulled back the sheets. "I'm growing rather fond of her soft parts."

"Speaking of," Riley said, peering at her heavy wardrobe draped over the back of a wooden chair. "Surely you're not going to have me wear all these dainty clothes while I visit your ranch? It hardly seems an appropriate outfit out on the range."

"Definitely not," Madame said, pulling open a drawer in the armoire and placing some new togs on the foot of the bed.

Riley glanced at each of the items, then she pulled the heavy canvas trousers over her knickers, securing them with a brass buckle belt.

"What are *these* for?" she said, holding up a pair of strange leather leggings cut off at the sides.

"Those are chaps," Madame said. "You wear them over the front of your pants to protect your legs from thorns and rope burns."

"Rope burns?" Riley said, tying the chaps around the front of her waist and admiring the rugged look in the dressing mirror.

"You're also going to have to learn how to ride a horse and rustle cattle. If you can't manage the rigors of the down-stairs saloon, maybe you can earn your keep out on the ranch."

"You're not wasting any time giving me the full immersion, are you?" Riley chuckled.

"It's a different lifestyle out here on the plains," Madame nodded. "You'll need to toughen up if you're going to survive more than a couple of weeks."

"What do I wear on *top*?" Riley said, grinning in the mirror at the appearance of her naked upper body with her rugged lower half. "Please tell me I don't have to wear that God-forsaken straight jacket anymore."

"That's only to impress the paying customers," Madame said. "You need to be far more comfortable out on the ranch."

She held up a checkered cotton long-sleeved shirt and when Riley pulled it on and buttoned up the front, she placed her hands under her free-hanging breasts, pinching her eyebrows.

"Am I supposed to wear it *au naturale*?" she said.

"Most women tie it at the bottom to support their breasts. You can wear a leather vest overtop if you wish to protect your modesty."

Riley unfastened the bottom three buttons of her shirt then tied a tight knot a few inches above her navel.

"What do you think?" she said, swinging around to show Bess her new outfit.

"Very sexy," Bess said, peering at her compressed cleavage. "But you might want to consider wearing the vest to keep your midsection from getting covered in dust."

Riley pulled the leather vest over her shoulders, nodding approvingly in the mirror.

"I'm starting to feel like a real cowboy," she grinned. "But something's definitely missing..."

Madame nodded, pulling a pair of women's cowboy boots out of the closet, and when Riley found they fit her perfectly, she beamed at herself in the mirror.

"Much better," she said. "I can't be a real cowgirl without authentic cowboy boots."

"True," Madame said, peering at Riley in the dressing mirror. "But you're still missing one thing."

She reached above the armoire, pulling a white felt cowboy hat off the top, placing it atop Riley's head. Riley tilted it to one side then angled her hips, feigning her best John Wayne imitation.

"Howdy, partner," she drawled, placing her hands on her hips. "Do I look like a real cowboy now?"

"A sexy-ass one, that's for sure," Bess said, peering at Riley's tight ass framed by the cutout of her chaps.

"A little *too* sexy, perhaps," Madame nodded, glancing down at Riley's hips.

"A real cowboy isn't complete until he has a six-shooter resting at his side. We'll complete the rest of the picture when we get you out to the ranch."

———

Riley rode out to the farmstead on the back of Madame's horse, holding on for dear life as she bucked and rocked atop the hard leather saddle. By the time she reached the ranch, her ass was sore and the insides of her legs were chafing. But the view to the west was magnificent, with the snow-capped Rockies rising above the rolling meadowland, where a group of scattered cattle grazed quietly.

"This is all *yours*?" Riley said, turning around to take in the endless vistas and the enormous sky.

"A thousand acres," Madame nodded, pointing toward the mountains. "Right up to the foothills. Just over that ridge is the newly created Yellowstone Park."

"It's gorgeous," Riley said, taking a deep breath of the fresh mountain air. "Why would you ever want to leave this place? It's a lot more peaceful than that noisy saloon."

"And a lot more *lonely*," Madame nodded. "A ranch is no place for a single woman. I've got a ranch hand to help me look after the place. I rather enjoy all the excitement of the saloon."

Madame peered toward one of the outbuildings, noticing a man leading a horse by a cord. She trotted up next to him then turned her body, sliding off the side of the horse and holding out her hand to help Riley dismount.

"This is Ben, my all-round ranch hand," Madame said, motioning toward the lanky cowboy. "Ben, this is my new saloon girl, Riley. She's new in these parts, and I was hoping you could help show her the ropes, in a manner of speaking."

"Of course," Ben said, tipping his hat toward Riley. "Where would you like to get started?"

Riley took a moment to appraise the handsome cowboy. He looked to be in his early thirties, with curly blond locks spilling out under his sandy-colored hat and piercing blue eyes, set above a lightly stubbled square jaw.

"Um," Riley stammered, momentarily taken aback by his Robert Redford looks. "I have no idea. Madame suggested I should learn how to shoot a gun..."

"Why don't you take Riley behind the stables to give her a little practice?" Madame said. "I'll fix us some lunch and later we can go for a ride together to explore the property."

"I'd like that," Riley said, referring more to the idea of taking the sexy cowboy behind the barn than riding the uncomfortable horse again.

"Right, then," Ben said, holding out his hand for Riley to follow him toward the shooting range. "Have you ever handled a gun before?"

"Not one as long and shiny as *that*," Riley smiled, glancing down at the six-shooter dangling at the side of Ben's hip next to the bulge in his pants.

5

———————

After Madame went inside the house to prepare lunch, Ben took Riley behind the barn, where he set up an impromptu shooting range with a bunch of liquor bottles propped up on a piece of barn siding.

"Just like in the movies," Riley nodded, peering at the familiar arrangement.

"The *what?*" Ben said.

"Oh nothing," Riley said, remembering all the comforts of modern life that had yet to be invented.

"Okay," Ben said, unholstering his pistol and moving behind Riley to place the gun in her hand. "It will likely be a bit of a shock for you to fire a gun for the first time. I'm going to steady your hand and help you aim."

He raised Riley's right hand, pointing the pistol at the row of bottles.

"If you want to be *accurate*, you'll need to learn how to use the gun sights to hit your targets."

"Isn't that the point of firing at something?" Riley said,

feeling Ben's crotch rubbing up against her ass. "To be accurate?"

"Yes, but sometimes you also need to be *fast*, depending on what you're shooting. First, we'll work on accuracy, then we'll worry about speed."

"Where are the gun sights?"

"If you look along the top of the barrel, you'll see two raised notches, one at the end and another closer to the trigger. Close your left eye and try to line up the sights with one of the bottles, then all you have to do is pull the trigger."

"Okay..." Riley said, following Ben's instructions while curling her finger through the loop next to the trigger. "Should I fire now?"

"Whenever you're ready," Ben said, holding her hand as she pointed the pistol.

Riley fired the gun and grunted when the bullet exploded from the chamber, pressing her body back against Ben.

"Uh!" she groaned, not accustomed to the heavy recoil from the firearm. "This hardly seems the sort of thing to be handled by a lady."

"It's alright," Ben said, caressing her shoulder reassuringly. "You get used to it pretty fast. Once you know how to counterbalance the recoil, it will become second nature."

"But I missed my target," Riley said, peering at the untouched row of bottles sitting thirty feet away.

"Hardly anybody hits their target the first time," Ben nodded. "Try again. This time, try holding the gun with *two* hands to steady your aim."

Riley did as Ben instructed, and as she lifted her other hand to grasp the handle, he lowered his palms, placing them softly on the sides of her hips.

"I'm not sure this is going to work any better," Riley said, her pulse racing from the feeling of his hands on her midsection.

"Try to steady your breathing before you shoot this time," he said. "The trick is to calm your nerves before you fire. Otherwise, your *body* will be in control of the outcome instead of your mind."

"Easier said than done," she said, feeling her underwear dampening from the sensation of Ben's bulging crotch against her ass.

"Slow and steady..." Ben said in a reassuring voice. "Set your stance to prepare for the recoil, then squeeze the trigger in one smooth motion."

Riley widened her legs a few inches and pressed her ass backwards as she bent her knees to prepare to fire. When she pulled the trigger, one of the bottles popped, exploding in a shower of glass.

"Woo-hoo!" she shouted, turning around to hug Ben.

He turned the barrel away from his body, then wrapped his arms around her, holding her firmly.

"Good girl," he said. "But one strike doesn't make you an expert. You've got to practice until it becomes second nature. Sometimes you'll need to fire more than one shot to neutralize your quarry."

"Okay," Riley said, turning back around and raising her gun toward the remaining bottles. "How many of these do I have to break before I get another hug?"

"*All* of them," Ben said. "Then maybe you'll get more than a hug."

"Okay then," Riley smiled. "I'll hold you to that."

She raised her other hand and steadied the gun, shifting into a semi-squat position while Ben peered down at her ass. When she fired the pistol, another bottle exploded then one by one, she picked off the rest of the bottles, moving from right to left.

"How about *that*?" Riley said, raising the barrel in front of her face and blowing the smoke like she'd seen in the movies.

"Very impressive," Ben said. "But those are some pretty easy targets, so close up. Your adversaries won't always make themselves so easy to hit."

"What's the typical distance between shooters in a duel?" Riley said, remembering what Bess had said about the way her husband died.

"One hundred paces," Ben said. "Though I'd hardly expect you to be challenged to a duel anytime soon."

"You never know," Riley frowned. "I've already had to defend my virtue twice in the last two days. I'll feel a lot safer with a gun in my hand."

"As you wish," Ben said, picking up the barn board and walking further out into the field to place the board on some rocks, picking up some stray bottles to set the target. When he returned to Riley's side, he took the revolver from her hand to reload it with six more bullets, spinning the cylinder to fill each chamber.

"You'll have to make a slight adjustment this time," he said, handing the loaded pistol back to her. "At a hundred yards, gravity begins to pull the bullet down. You'll need to aim a fraction of an inch higher to hit your target from this distance."

"Okay," Riley said, resuming her stance and squinting her eye to aim the pistol at one of the bottles in the distance.

When she fired, the bottles remained undisturbed, and she shook her head in frustration.

"It's okay," Ben said, moving closer to her. "It takes a little bit of trial and error to take into account the effects of gravity and cross winds. Pick up a handful of grass and toss it into the air to check the direction of the breeze."

Riley picked up a clump of grass and when she threw it in the air, it drifted gently a few inches to her left side.

"You'll need to aim a few millimeters to the right this time," Ben nodded. "Try it again."

Riley adjusted her aim as Ben instructed, and her next shot broke one of the bottles. Then, just as she'd done the first time, she moved her hands from right to left, picking off the rest of the bottles in quick succession.

"How about that?" Riley said, turning towards Ben with a huge smile. "Maybe you should start calling me Billy the Kid."

"Billy the Kid earned his reputation as a gunfighter shooting real people, not just bottles," Ben chuckled. "If you want to have a chance of holding your own against someone like that, you'll have to be fast, not just accurate. And be ready to shoot a real *person*, not just a bunch of inanimate objects."

"How do I prepare for something like that?"

Ben paused for a moment, then pulled a roll of newspaper from his back pocket, tacking it to the side of the barn. Then he pulled out his knife, cutting out the rough shape of a person.

"That looks a lot easier to hit," Riley grinned.

"Not when they're shooting back at you," Ben said. "Stand back a hundred paces and try it again."

After Ben reloaded her pistol, Riley strutted out one hundred steps into the field, then turned around and aimed her gun at the outline on the barn while Ben moved further to the side.

"What part of his body should I aim for?" Riley said.

"At that distance, you just want to clip him anywhere

you can. If you wound him, you'll have a better chance to finish the job with your second shot. Aim for his torso. There's a better chance of striking him there."

Riley raised her pistol and steadied her aim, and when she fired the gun, a puff of dust blew off the side of the shed. Ben walked up to the newspaper and placed his finger over the right shoulder of the figure to indicate where her bullet had landed.

"Not bad," he said. "Now try firing from your hip, and faster. You won't always have time to aim so carefully when someone is firing back at you."

After Ben stepped further off to the side, Riley positioned her pistol at the side of her hips like she'd seen in so many Westerns, then she quickly raised her hand, firing the remaining five bullets. When she emptied the chamber, Ben walked up to the makeshift target, nodding his head slowly.

"You're a natural," he smiled. "I think you killed him."

"Really?" Riley said, scampering up to the side of the barn to inspect her handiwork. When she peered at the figure, all but one of her bullets had found their mark on the man's upper body.

"Yippee!" she said, jumping up and down while she hugged Ben. "I'm a real gunslinger now."

"You're beginning to shoot like one," he nodded. "Let's hope you only have to shoot targets on the side of a *barn* instead of the real thing. I'd hate to see that pretty body of yours filled with holes."

"Oh?" Riley said, pressing her body against Ben's. "I could use one of my holes filled right about now..."

6

———

Ben flipped Riley around, pressing her up against the side of the barn. While they kissed each other, he unbuckled her pants, pulling her bloomers down below her knees, then he unzipped his trousers, raising her ass with the palms of his hands. Riley wrapped her legs around his hips and when he thrust his hard cock inside her, she gasped.

"Mmm," she purred. "I like the feel of *this* gun more than your six-shooter."

"Yeah?" Ben panted. "Do you think you can handle this one as well as the other?"

"It's been a while," she grunted, bouncing off the creaking sideboards of the barn. "But you seem to have the matter well in hand."

"I've been wanting to squeeze this ass of yours from the moment I laid eyes on you," Ben said, gripping her cheeks tightly while he slammed her against the barn with each powerful thrust.

"And I've been dying to feel that gun of yours ever since you trotted out the horse with a big bulge in your pants."

"Which one?" he grunted.

"Isn't it obvious?" Riley groaned, biting his lower lip. "I haven't been fucked like this in a long time."

"No?" Ben said. "They don't have rough and tumble cowboys where you come from?"

"Only in the movies," Riley shuddered, squeezing Ben's hips harder as he made one final powerful thrust.

Ben paused for a moment, holding Riley up against the side of the barn while they both came down from their highs, then he slowly lowered her to the ground, angling his dick in his pants while he closed the zipper.

"Madame wasn't kidding when she said you were an all-round ranch hand," Riley chuckled, pulling up her trousers and retying them around her waist. "What *other* talents do you have that you haven't told me about?"

"I'm just a simple cowboy," Ben grinned. "Steers and steeds are pretty much all I tend to these days."

"And the occasional wandering *filly*," Riley smiled.

"If the need arises," Ben nodded.

"Mmm," Riley said, lifting her nose at the scent of cooking meat coming from the main house. "All this exercise has gotten me hungry. Are you as famished as I am?"

"Always," Ben said, nodding for Riley to lead the way.

When they opened the door to Madame's ranch house, they saw her leaning over a wood stove in a corner of the living room, stirring a steaming pot.

"That smells heavenly," Riley said, walking closer to the pot to see what she was cooking.

"Have you worked up an appetite from all that target practice?" Madame said.

"Among other things," Riley nodded. "Can I help you with anything?"

"I'm almost done," Madame said, dipping a ladle into the

pot and pouring the contents onto three porcelain plates. Then she carried the plates over to a thick oak table, motioning for Ben and Riley to have a seat.

"Beef stew," Riley nodded. "Just like my mother used to make."

"I hope you like it," Madame said, slicing a piece of meat. "Everything's grown right here on the ranch."

"Mmm," Riley said, biting into the tender flesh flavored with potatoes and beans. "How many cattle do you keep on the property?"

"Four hundred or so," Madame said. "It's relatively small by Wyoming standards."

"That's a lot of cows for one cowboy to keep track of," Riley said, turning toward Ben. "Even one as able-bodied as Ben."

"They pretty much look after themselves," Madame nodded, peering at the two of them with a suspicious look. "There's plenty of wild grass for them to eat and the property is fenced to keep them from straying. We'll go for a ride after lunch, where I'll teach you to ride a horse. How did she do on the shooting range?"

"She's a natural," Ben smiled. "A veritable Billy the Kid."

"Good," Madame said. "Because if her first two days at the saloon is any judge, she may need to fight off the advances of these cowboys with more than a broom."

After lunch, Madame and Ben escorted Riley out to the barn, where they saddled up one of the smaller mares, teaching her how to ride the animal using a tether in the fenced paddock. After fifteen minutes or so, Riley seemed to be getting the hang of it, and they opened the gate, heading out in the direction of the foothills to inspect the herd.

"This is pretty cool," Riley beamed, thrilled at the feel of riding a horse through the tall grass while admiring the beautiful view. "A girl could get used to this life pretty quickly. Are you sure you don't need another ranch hand?"

"I need you more at the *saloon*," Madame said. "Cows can look after themselves, but unfortunately, cowboys need constant care and feeding."

"Among other things," Riley smiled, stealing a glance at Ben atop his spotted stallion.

"Careful you don't hold the reins too tightly," Madame admonished, trying to refocus Riley's attention. "The trick to riding a horse properly is using your *lower* body more than your hands. Use your legs to steer the horse and control her speed, then simply relax your shoulders to move in unison with her."

"Right," Riley said, feeling her pussy rubbing up against the front stub of the saddle. "Use the lower half."

As the trio trotted around the perimeter of the ranch, Ben paused at one of the corners, noticing a tipped fence post. He dismounted his horse, then righted the post, packing some extra dirt around the base with a heavy rock.

"How did *that* happen?" Riley said, watching Ben's sinewy arm muscles flexing as he pounded the earth.

"Who knows?" he said. "Maybe it was a bear wandering down from the mountains looking for some easy pickings. This sort of thing happens pretty often on a ranch of this size."

Riley peered at the thin strands connecting the posts, then shook her head.

"What keeps people from stealing the cattle when you're not looking, especially at night? It seems simple enough to cut the barbed wire to let them escape."

"Cattle rustling is punishable by hanging," Madame said. "All of our cattle are branded, so everyone knows who they belong to."

"Assuming you can find them after they go missing," Riley said, noticing Ben's stallion sniffing her horse's behind.

"That's what sheriffs and posses are for," Madame said. "Most rustlers don't get very far with slow-moving cattle. The trail is pretty easy to follow, what with all the cow droppings and trampled grass."

Riley's eyes widened, watching Ben's horse's penis swelling from its sheath, flopping inches from the ground.

"It's nice to know that sheriff is good for *something*," she said. "Apparently he's more interested in protecting *cows* than women."

"Yes," Madame said. "It takes something pretty serious to get him off his duff. He seems more interested in keeping the peace than defending a woman's virtue. Sometimes I think he gets a little too friendly with that rabble-rising lot."

"Speaking of *virtue*," Riley said, noticing Ben's horse snorting and bucking up and down. "I think your horse has some amorous intentions of his own."

"He's not used to being out on the range with a *mare*," Ben nodded, hopping on the animal and steering him back toward the stables. "Normally the Madame and I ride stallions and geldings."

"What's a gelding?"

"A castrated male."

"Ouch," Riley said, peering between the legs of Madame's horse. "That doesn't sound very pleasant."

"They're clipped when they're young," Madame smiled. "After the initial shock, they don't know what they're missing."

"If you say so," Riley said, scrunching up her face at the thought.

7

———

When the three riders returned to the paddock, Madame and Riley went into the house to clean up, while Ben took the horses into the barn to feed and water them.

"Are you enjoying life on the range?" Madame said, fetching a bowl of water to clean her face and hands.

"It's a far cry from my life in Boston," Riley nodded. "But I like the open spaces and the fresh smell of the air."

"It seems that's not the *only* thing attracting your interest out here on the ranch," she smiled. "You and Ben seem to have hit it off pretty fast."

"Yes," Riley said. "He's been very helpful. Like you said, he has many talents."

"Not to mention his handsome features and muscular physique."

"Oh?" Riley said, turning to inspect some old photographs lining the wall of Madame's living room. "I hadn't noticed. Is this a picture of your husband?"

"Yes," Madame said, strolling over to stand beside Riley.

"He died of typhoid fever not long after we built this ranch. It was too lonely for me to stay here by myself, which is why I invested in the saloon."

"You don't lean on Ben occasionally for some additional companionship?"

"I don't like to mix business with pleasure. He's got his hands full enough around here, what with the cattle and the horses and the rustlers."

"So it would seem," Riley said, not yet ready to disclose her secret tryst with the handsome cowboy behind the barn.

"Would you like me to warm up some water for a bath?" Madame said. "You're covered in dust from the ride in the field."

"That would be nice, thank you," Riley nodded.

While Madame boiled some water on the wood stove, Riley walked around the interior of her home, peering at the faded black and white photographs lining the wall.

"These remind me of the old photographs my grandmother used to show me," she said, smiling at the quaint pictures of people standing next to old rocking chairs and wash basins on the front porch.

"Oh?" Madame said. "I didn't know they even had photographs that long ago. It's a fairly recent invention–"

"Yes," Riley said, remembering that she'd traveled a hundred and fifty years into the past from the present day. "They were pictures of her later in life..."

"Come," Madame said, pouring the last of the water into the tub and dipping her hand in to test the temperature. "Let me help you out of those dusty clothes."

"Of course," Riley said, strolling over to the bathtub, where Madame unbuttoned her vest and shirt, hanging them over a post in the corner.

When she unbuckled Riley's pants and she stepped out of them, Madame noticed the rash on her lower back and the splinters on her buttocks from her earlier pounding against the barn.

"I see Ben wasn't just showing you how to handle a *pistol*," Madame said, rubbing her fingers over her cheeks.

"Um, yes," Riley said, finally giving up the charade. "He was helping me aim the gun and one thing led to another. I hope you don't mind..."

"Of course not," Madame said, holding Riley's hand as she stepped into the tub. "I run a brothel after all. I'm hardly shocked when two people want to have sex."

After Riley lowered herself into the steaming water, Madame began to unbutton her own clothing, placing her garments on the rack next to Riley's.

"You'll be joining me?"

"Of course," Madame said. "I'm just as soiled as you are from the ride on the range. Hot water is a precious commodity out here. We have to take every opportunity to share our limited resources whenever we can."

While Madame lifted her leg to step into the other side of the tub, Riley studied her body before she immersed herself under the surface. She had a surprisingly firm and supple figure for someone her age. Estimating her at roughly forty-five years, her breasts were full and buoyant, with round hips and muscular thighs that revealed her active life on the ranch. As she slid under the water, pressing her naked ass against Riley's, Riley felt a throbbing in her pussy, remembering the sexy encounter she'd had with Bess the previous day.

"There now," Madame purred, peering at her with a flushed face. "Doesn't that feel better?"

"Just what I need for my aching muscles," Riley nodded. "I had no idea riding a horse was so much work."

"You'll hurt a lot more *tomorrow*," Madame said, caressing Riley's swollen feet from being cramped in the tight cowboy boots all day. "You're using your thigh and buttock muscles in an entirely new way. It's going to take a little while for them to become accustomed to riding a horse."

"Not to mention a well-hung *cowboy*," Riley grinned.

After the two women finished their long bath, Madame patted Riley dry with a soft towel, then turned her around to inspect her scraped backside.

"The hot water softened up your skin around the splinters," she nodded. "But you've still got a few that need to be removed. Why don't you lie down on my bed while I fetch some tweezers and see if I can get you a little more tidied up?"

Madame led Riley into her rear bed chamber, then she pulled back the bedspread, easing Riley face-down onto the firm mattress. Then she walked over to a dresser on the wall, opening a drawer to remove her toiletry kit. When she returned to the bed, she kneeled on the mattress, resting her naked hips over the back of Riley's butt while she carefully pulled the slivers out of her back. When she finished, she swiped the pieces of wood off the back of her ass, placing the tweezers on the footboard at the end of the bed.

"There," she said, pressing her warm pussy against Riley's crimson ass. "Good as new. Next time, you and Ben might want to consider rolling in the *hay* instead of against the side of the barn. It's still a bit scratchy, but at least you won't end up with any more splinters."

"Mmm," Riley grunted, rolling her hips softly against Madame's moistening sex. "I think I'd rather stay here in this soft bed."

"Oh?" Madame said, rocking her hips against Riley's butt. "Do you also like the touch of a woman once in a while?"

"Absolutely," Riley said, sliding her hands down her side to caress Madame's thighs.

"I *thought* Bess seemed to have more than a passing interest in you this morning," Madame nodded. "I suppose it's a good thing I've got you sleeping in a brothel. You'll have your choice of any girl in the saloon before you decide you've had your fill."

"What makes you think I'll satisfy my desires any time soon?" Riley said, flipping over to gaze into Madame's eyes, caressing her swelling teats with the back of her hand.

"I don't know," Madame smiled, rocking her mound against Riley's as she pulled Riley's hands around her breasts. "There's something about you and your mysterious history. I think you're an itinerant traveler, like the tumbleweed that bounces through town."

"Well, I do like a good *bouncing* once in a while," Riley said, sitting up to kiss Madame while they pressed their tits together.

Madame moaned and pressed Riley back onto the mattress, then she lifted her right leg, scissoring her hips between Riley's thighs.

"So do I," Madame grunted, mashing her wet pussy against Riley's while she pulled her leg higher above her body.

"I thought you didn't like to mix business with *pleasure*?"

Riley smiled, watching Madame's tits swaying as she fucked her from above.

"You're still on probation," Madame groaned, gaping her mouth open in pleasure while their pussies slapped loudly together. "I still haven't decided if I'm going to keep you."

8

———

The next day, Riley and Madame returned to town, where Riley resumed her duties as a waitress in the saloon. After a long day of fending off the advances of leering cowboys, she retired to her room upstairs, nestling in beside Bess, who was sleeping peacefully in the bed.

"All done already?" Bess murmured, rolling over to press her body against Riley's. "What time is it?"

"Madame let me off a bit early," Riley said, slipping her thigh between Bess's legs. "I think she was worried I was going to dump another beer over one of those randy cowboys."

"Are they up to their usual shenanigans?" Bess said, kissing Riley's neck as Riley pulled her knee toward her pussy.

"It never ends," Riley nodded. "But at least now I carry a pistol up my garter if they get too frisky."

"And you know how to use it?"

"I spent most of the day practicing with Madame's ranch hand yesterday."

"Mmm," Bess hummed. "I hear he's dreamy. Is that the *only* thing he taught you to use?"

"Let's just say he knows how to fire more than a six-shooter," Riley grinned. "And I've got the splinters on my ass to prove it."

"Oh?" Bess said, sliding down under the covers to caress Riley's backside. "He took you behind the barn and had his way with you, did he?"

"Yes, and he's hung almost as well as his *horse*."

Bess slowly pushed Riley's knees apart, lowering her head toward her pussy.

"Does he know how to do *this* too?" she said, sliding her tongue up Riley's dripping slit.

"We didn't get that far," Riley panted, pulling Bess's head harder against her vulva. "But *your* face is better suited for that sort of thing."

As Riley began to moan and rock her hips against Bess's lips, suddenly they heard a loud scream coming from down the hall. She sat up quickly in the bed, flinging her eyes wide open.

"What was that?" she said.

"It's probably just one of the girls putting on a show for her customer. The johns like it when they pretend to like it."

Riley turned her head to listen to the sound of loud slapping and squealing.

"That doesn't sound to me like she's *enjoying* it."

She got out of bed and pulled on her bloomers, drawing her new pistol from its holster.

"I'm going to check it out."

Bess scrambled out of bed and grabbed Riley's arm to stop her from barging out the door.

"You should leave well enough alone," she said. "It's

normal for some of the customers to get a little rough. It's part of the job."

"Not where *I* come from," Riley said, swinging open the door and walking in the direction of the disturbance.

When she got to the edge of the room, she could hear the distinct sound of a fist slamming flesh, and the pleas of a young woman begging for the man to stop hitting her.

"No!" the girl cried. "You're *hurting* me!"

"Then bend over and let me fuck your ass like a good little whore," the man said.

Riley pounded on the door, trying to turn the handle, but it was firmly locked.

"What's going on in there?" she shouted.

"Mind your own business, bitch," the man shouted back. "This is between me and the trollop."

"I don't think so," Riley said, shaking the door loudly.

When it didn't budge, she stepped back a few feet, then kicked the door as hard as she could beside the latch with the heel of her foot. The flimsy panel flung open, and the same man who'd accosted her on her first day turned around to glare at her.

"*You* again," he sneered. "You have a bad habit of showing up in the wrong places."

"*You're* the one who's forgotten his place," she said, pointing the gun at the man's midsection like Ben had taught her.

"You little tramp," the man said, taking a step forward. "I'll show you how to handle a gun–"

Riley quickly lowered her pistol, firing a bullet into the floorboards between the man's legs.

"Stop right there, or the next one will separate you from your balls," she sneered.

The man paused for a moment, then glanced up when

he saw Madame appear behind Riley in front of the room's entrance.

"What the *fuck*, Madame?" the man said. "Since when do your girls break into your private rooms while we're doing our business?"

"That depends what kind of business you're conducting," Madame said, noticing the welts and bruises on the girl's face. "You know we don't abide by any violence against our girls. I think it's time for you to leave now, Amos."

"Fine by me," Amos said, picking up his clothes lying on the floor. "This bitch doesn't do as she's told, anyhow."

After he pulled on his pants and wrapped his gun belt around his waist, he paused beside Riley.

"As for you," he sneered. "That's the last time you'll fire a pistol at me. "I challenge you to a duel tomorrow at noon. We'll see who's the quicker draw around here."

After Amos left the room, Riley turned toward Madame with a surprised look on her face.

"Is he serious?" she said. "Am I expected to honor this absurd demand?"

"Unfortunately, yes," Madame said. "If you pull a gun on someone, he's perfectly within his rights to challenge you to a contest."

"Even if I was defending someone from harm?"

"That's how people settle their differences around here," Madame nodded.

"What about the *law*?" Riley said. "Aren't people held to account for their actions with due process?"

"Only for something as serious as cattle rustling or killing an unarmed man," Madame said. "I'll talk to the sheriff to plead your case, but I don't see any other way around it. You're going to have to face him in the town square and settle it in the way of the west."

Bess scurried up beside Madame, buttoning up her clothes.

"You'd better practice some more then," she said, peering at Riley with a worried expression. "I'm not sure one day on the farm is going to cut it."

Jesus, Riley thought, suddenly missing the civilized world she'd left behind in Boston. *Where's an honest judge and a lawman when you need one?*

9

That night, Riley could barely sleep. All she could think about was visions of being plugged full of holes while the sneering cowboy stood over her lifeless body. By dawn, she was covered in a cold sweat, dreading the thought of having to face the more experienced gunman. As she peered up toward the top of the valence where she'd hidden her time machine, she thought about escaping through the portal to another time and place.

But how could she know the next stop would be any less violent and dangerous? Both the pirate ship and the western frontier town were full of scoundrels and weapons she was unaccustomed to handling. She knew that eventually she'd have to stand up for herself and learn the customs of each period if she was going to survive these time travel adventures.

Bess suddenly rolled over, feeling Riley's leg shaking in nervousness.

"You're dripping *wet*," she said, sitting up. "Did you get any sleep at *all* last night?"

"How could I?" Riley said. "I'm about to go face to face with someone who's been shooting a gun his whole life. I've barely had time to practice hitting the side of a barn."

"But Madame said you'd gotten quite skilled at hitting your targets?"

"Yes," Riley nodded. "Empty liquor bottles and paper figures. This target shoots back."

There was a soft tap on the door and Madame stuck her head in, noticing the two women were awake.

"I see you're up already," she said, closing the door behind her and sitting on the side of the bed. "Have you been summoning your strength for the coming duel?"

"I'm not sure *strength* is going to help me much," Riley said, crossing her arms to still her shaking muscles. "Did you talk with the sheriff? Is there any chance at a reprieve?"

"It was just as I feared," Madame said, placing her hand over Riley's wrist. "The rules are quite clear in this kind of situation. When you draw a gun on an unarmed man, he has the right to demand a duel."

"What about the assault on the *girl*?"

"There were no witnesses," Madame said. "It's one person's word against the other."

"But I heard it on the other side of the door," Riley said. "What about the bruises on her face?"

"Unfortunately, we can't prove that he was the one who administered them. The judge won't allow hearsay as sufficient evidence to convict a person."

Riley shook her head, barely believing the predicament she'd gotten herself into.

"That guy's a piece of work," she said. "He's too cowardly even to admit abusing a defenseless woman."

"At least you have a chance to even the score now," Madame said, squeezing Riley's arm. "All you have to do is calm your nerves and follow the instructions Ben taught you."

Riley suddenly sat up, remembering the handsome ranch hand who'd steadied her arm and helped guide her pistol.

"Will he be coming to watch the contest? I could use his steady hand and comforting advice right about now."

"There's been some trouble on the ranch," Madame said. "He's going to have to stay to keep an eye on the horses and cattle."

"What *kind* of trouble?"

"More fallen fence posts. And some of the cattle seem to be missing."

Riley furrowed her forehead with her mind temporarily distracted from the matter at hand.

"Will the sheriff be going to investigate?" she said. "Will they be forming a posse to chase the bandits?"

Madame shook her head.

"He has to stay to supervise the duel. Someone needs to make sure no one takes unfair advantage."

"Like shooting a woman who's just learned how to fire a gun?"

"I actually think *you* have the advantage in this situation," she said. "He'll be underestimating your capabilities and trying to be first on the draw. But if he misses, you'll have more time to line him up and make your first shot count."

"If he misses?"

"It's common for the first shot to miss," Madame nodded. "That's why there's six bullets in the cylinder. Your best chance is to try and remain calm."

"That's easy for you to say," Riley grunted. "You're not the one on the other end of a speeding bullet."

As the noon hour approached, people began to line both sides of the main street, curious to see how the newcomer would hold her own against the rough and tumble cowboy. Even the working girls from the second floor joined Madame and Bess outside the front entrance of the saloon, eager to show support for Riley.

"Looks like the whole town has come out to watch this spectacle," Riley said, standing beside them.

"This sort of thing doesn't happen very often," Madame nodded. "Especially with a woman involved."

"I seem to have a habit of sticking my foot in places it doesn't belong," Riley said. "I guess I come from a different time where men and women are treated equally."

"At least you'll have a chance to be treated equal for a brief moment. It doesn't get much more equal than two people fighting to the death using the same weapons."

Riley peered across the dusty street toward the sheriff's office, noticing Amos standing on the veranda, chatting with James.

"Except he appears to have *two* guns on his belt, whereas I've only got one," she frowned.

"I don't think more guns will make much of a difference in a battle like this," Madame said. "It won't take more than two or three bullets to settle the score. You've got six rounds in your pistol—just make sure to use them wisely."

"I don't even know if I'll be able to raise my *hand*, let alone my gun, I'm shaking so hard right now."

"It's okay, honey," Bess said, wrapping her arms around Riley to still her quivering body. "The good guys always win in the end. I've got a good feeling about this. Just remember what that jerk did to poor Julie. That should give you the courage to stand up to him."

"Yes," she said, glancing at Julie's bruised cheeks. "Let's see how well he does when he's facing someone who can hit back."

"That's the attitude," Madame smiled, noticing the sheriff nodding as the church bell struck noon. "You can do this. Just keep your nerves and wait for him to make the first mistake."

"Right," Riley said, feeling her heart beginning to pound out of her chest. "Wait for him to take the first shot..."

As Amos and the sheriff strolled out to the middle of the street, Bess grabbed Riley's arm, kissing her on the side of the cheek.

"Knock him dead," she said with a lopsided smile. "Let's show these cowboys who's the boss around here."

As Riley walked out to join the other men in the center of the street, her legs felt like Jello, barely able to withstand the weight of her slender figure, feeling like a ton of bricks. When she approached Amos, he glared at with a sinister sneer.

"Right then," the sheriff said, glancing at the two opponents. "You'll start with your backs against one another then take fifty paces in opposite directions. When you turn around, each of you must pause for five seconds while the other sets his position. The contest is over when one of the fighters falls or kneels in defeat."

"Right," Amos snickered. "There's no chance of that. This will be a fight to the death."

Riley peered at the sheriff with an empty expression, feeling nothing but disdain for the man. She found it telling that he'd used the masculine pronoun to describe the rules of the duel.

Apparently, it's going to take another hundred years for men to see women as equals, she thought.

The sheriff motioned for the two opponents to turn around then they both began walking in opposite directions. Riley could barely count out the number of steps, with her breath catching in her throat. But at least she felt a degree of comfort knowing there were witnesses to prevent Amos from shooting her while her back was turned.

When she counted fifty paces and turned around, she saw that Amos was already standing facing her, with his right hand resting over his pistol. As she lowered her hand to the top of her six-shooter, the five seconds seem to pass by in agonizing slow motion.

Suddenly, without warning, Amos reached for his gun early and pointed it toward Riley, firing a puff a smoke from the barrel. Riley's hat tipped over onto the ground and in the shock of the near-miss, she pulled her gun from her holster, aiming at her opponent's midsection as another bullet whizzed past her ear. Her bullet caught Amos in his right shoulder, and he flinched, dropping his gun.

As he reached over his hip for his second gun, Riley grasped her pistol firmly with two hands, lining Amos up through the sights. When she fired her second shot, it landed squarely in the middle of his chest, and he peered back at her for a moment in disbelief before crumpling to the ground.

The crowd stood in stunned silence, waiting to see if Amos was dead, but he lay in the dirt, motionless. When it was obvious the duel was over, the girls from the front of the saloon rushed out to surround Riley, hugging her ecstatically.

"You did it!" Bess said, jumping up and down. "You're the first woman to beat a man in a gun duel!"

"Three cheers for woman's liberation," Riley grunted, feeling a sickening sensation in her stomach from killing another person.

"Woman's what?" Madame said, removing the shaking gun from Riley's hand.

"Let's just say this won't be the *first* time a woman matches a man's deeds in history," Riley said.

Bess suddenly eased her grip on Riley, squinting behind her toward the end of the street.

"Is that *Ben* from Madame's ranch?" she said, furrowing her brow with a worried expression. "He looks hurt."

Riley swung around, peering into the distance. A spotted horse trotted toward them with a man slumped forward onto its neck with his hand hanging over its flanks, dripping blood.

"Ben!" she screamed, rushing toward the injured man.

10

The women rushed up to Ben's horse and pulled him off, laying him gently in the sand. Riley darted her eyes over his body looking for signs of the wound, and when she pulled his vest away, she saw a dark stain over the right side of his abdomen. When she unbuttoned his shirt, she noticed a deep hole dripping blood.

"Someone get a *doctor*!" she screamed, peering around her frantically.

Madame leaned over Ben, brushing the sweat from his brow.

"Who did this to you?" she said.

"The Adams gang," Ben grunted, struggling to breathe. "I caught them cutting a hole in the fence and when I tried to stop them, they ambushed me."

"That's the same group that accosted you at the saloon the other day," Madame nodded, turning toward Riley.

"Did you see in which direction they headed?" the sheriff said, walking up beside Ben.

"Southwest toward Colorado," Ben said, wincing in pain.

The town doctor pushed his way through the crowd, then knelt beside Ben. He took one look at the wound and shook his head.

"He's been shot in the liver," he said. "I'm afraid there's nothing I can do."

"Oh Ben," Riley sobbed, leaning her head down onto his chest. "You beautiful man. Thank you for being patient with me and helping me learn how to fire a gun."

"Did you win the contest?" he said with a half-hearted smile.

"Yes," Riley said. "I did just as you told me. I aimed for the big parts, then lined him up in the sights to finish him off."

"Good girl," Ben said, raising his arm to clasp Riley's hand.

Then he suddenly coughed, spitting up blood. As tears began to stream down Riley's face, she watched the life drain out of his eyes until his head slumped over to the side. She paused for a moment, then she stood up briskly, facing the sheriff.

"This is all *your* fault!" she said, pounding her fists onto his chest. "You stood by in the saloon watching those bastards molest me, then you failed to help Ben when he needed it."

"We had more pressing matters to attend to," James said, grabbing hold of Riley's wrists to stop her flailing.

"Are you going to chase the men responsible?" Riley said. "You can't let them get away with this!"

"I'll form a posse right away," the sheriff nodded. "But there's no guarantee we'll find them if they had a big enough head start."

"I want to go with you," Riley said.

"A posse's no place for a lady," James said. "There's likely to be more trouble when we find them and no accounting for how much shooting."

"I'm not a lady!" Riley shouted. "I'm a *woman*. And I think I've already demonstrated that I'm more than capable of handling a gun."

"Let *us* take care of this," James said. "You and the madame had best head back out to the ranch to prevent any more of your livestock from straying. We'll return when we find those responsible."

A fter the sheriff galloped out of town with a group of five other men, Riley turned toward Madame, wrinkling her forehead.

"There's something about that man that I don't trust," she said. "I think we should head out to the ranch to conduct our own investigation. He didn't sound very confident in his abilities to apprehend the criminals."

"You might be right," Madame said. "I know an Indian who might be able to help us follow the tracks."

She looked up at an bespeckled man who peered down at Ben's body solemnly.

"Will you take care of Ben's body while we're away, Eugene?" she said. "I'd like to give him a proper burial out on the ranch."

"Of course, Madame," the undertaker said.

"Can I go with you?" Bess said, stepping forward to stand beside Riley. "The more guns you have, the better."

"I think it's best you stay here," Madame said. "Watch over the rest of the girls and tell Clarence to keep an eye out in case the Adams gang circles back. With the sheriff out of town, there's no telling what additional mischief they might get into."

"Don't worry," Bess nodded. "If those bastards dare show their faces again in this town, we'll show them some real frontier justice."

After Riley and Madame saddled up their horses and headed back in the direction of the ranch, Riley peered over at Madame with a worried expression on her face.

"Do you really think we have a chance at catching those outlaws who killed Ben?"

"It depends on how far they've gotten," Madame nodded. "But my Indian friend has considerable experience with this sort of thing. If anybody can find them, he can."

After a few miles, they came upon an Indian settlement, and Madame dismounted to enter one of the teepees. A few minutes later, she emerged with a middle-aged Indian man, who fetched a horse with a patterned blanket draped over its back.

"This is Grey Cloud," Madame said, introducing the Indian to Riley. "And this is my friend Riley, who'll be joining us on the search."

"Pleased to meet you, Riley," the Indian man said in halting English.

When the trio got to the ranch, they found the hole in the fence and after repairing the barbed wire to prevent the escape of any more animals, they followed Grey Cloud in the direction of the foothills while he peered down at the ground. After an hour or so, he stopped his horse and dismounted, brushing his fingers softly over the earth.

"What is it?" Madame said. "Have you picked up the trail?"

"There are fresh tracks from a group of five or six horses," he nodded. "It joins a much larger track with many cattle and other horses."

"Those must be the tracks of the posse," Madame nodded. "The sheriff must have picked up on the rustlers' trail and taken pursuit."

Grey Cloud lifted a stick, pushing over a fresh pile of dung.

"They were here no more than thirty minutes ago," he said. "It won't be long before we catch up with them."

The group continued their pursuit for a few more miles, then Grey Cloud lifted his hand, stopping his horse again while he peered at the earth.

"Why are we stopping?" Madame said, looking at Grey Cloud with a puzzled expression.

"Something's not right," he said, shaking his head as he peered at the ground. "The posse's tracks have joined the cattle tracks, but the spacing of the hooves indicates the group has slowed to a walk."

"What do you think that means?" Madame said.

"I'm not sure," the Indian said. "But if the posse was really trying to capture the bandits, they would have stopped to engage them or continued the chase. These tracks almost make it seem like they've joined forces."

"Joined forces?" Madame said, furrowing her brow. "Why would they do that?"

"I knew we couldn't trust that bastard," Riley said, shaking her head. "Ever since I saw him laughing with the other men at the saloon, I've questioned his integrity. It's almost as if that duel was *staged* as a distraction to leave Ben fending for himself on the ranch."

"If you're right about that," Madame said. "We're going to have to be careful approaching them more closely. There's only three of us and God knows how many of them."

"I think we should walk the rest of the way," Grey Cloud nodded, lifting his nose in the air, smelling the scent of the nearby herd. "They look to be holed up in that gully over the next ridge. Let's hide our horses here in the bush and approach their camp on foot."

"Okay," Madame said. "I suppose that makes the most sense. But we'll have to be careful when we get closer. If the sheriff is really in cahoots with these outlaws, there's no telling what they'll do if we discover their secret."

As dusk began to fall over the foothills, the threesome crept toward a column of smoke rising up from the gully. When they got closer to the campfire, they paused behind a clump of sagebrush, parting the branches slowly. About a hundred feet away, they saw the sheriff and his posse sitting around the fire with the group from the saloon as the herd of cattle grazed quietly nearby.

"You say that girl slew Amos with two shots?" the ringleader said to James.

"He drew first," the sheriff nodded. "But when he missed with his first shot, she clipped him in the shoulder. He didn't have time to get off another round before she hit him square in his chest."

"Wherever she's from," the first man said. "She seems to know what she's doing."

"We'll have to watch out for her," James nodded. "She can cause more trouble for us if we don't find a way to neutralize her."

"I can think of a way to neutralize her," the man who groped Riley in the bar snickered. "I'll be happy to finish what I started a few days ago."

"It's better we just make her *disappear*," James said. "She doesn't seem to have any family in these parts. Nobody will miss her if she leaves the same way she came."

"And what will be the *price* of this silence?" the ring-leader said, turning toward James.

"Let's see," the sheriff paused. "Four hundred head of cattle at roughly one hundred dollars apiece comes to forty thousand. I think ten thousand should be sufficient compensation for turning a blind eye to your nefarious ways."

Riley gasped when she realized the sheriff was in on the plan the whole time, shifting her weight and snapping a branch underfoot. The cattle rustlers peered in their direction, standing up and raising their weapons in alarm.

"You go now!" Grey Cloud whispered, motioning for Riley and Madame to head back toward the horses. "I'll keep them distracted while you get away."

Madame peered at the Indian for a moment, then she grabbed Riley's hand, rushing off in the other direction. A few moments later, they heard some shouting behind them as Grey Cloud began flinging arrows at the band from his hiding place in the bushes.

"Indians!" someone shouted. "Circle around from the other side to see if we can trap them!"

While Madame and Riley untethered their horses and began galloping back in the direction of Cody, Riley turned toward Madame, shaking her head.

"Will Grey Cloud be alright?" she grunted, trying not to fall off her bouncing horse.

"He knows these hills better than anyone," Madame nodded. "He should be able to escape under cover of darkness. But we've got more important matters to worry about. We need to find a way to *protect* you when we get back to town."

11

———

When Madame and Riley returned to town, the first place they went was to see the mayor. They weren't sure when James would return, but when he did, they knew some changes would have to be made. When they entered the mayor's office, he was resting in his chair, reading the local newspaper.

"Madame," he said, sitting up. "Have you made any progress finding the bandits who stole your cattle?"

"Yes," Madame said. "But it won't be as easy as we thought to retrieve them."

"Did the sheriff and his posse catch up to them?"

"That's the problem," Madame nodded. "When we located them, we found that he'd arranged a deal for their escape."

"How do you mean?" the mayor said, rising up out of his chair.

"We overheard him taking a bribe to let them get away. I'm afraid our sheriff can no longer be trusted."

"That's a very serious matter, indeed," the mayor said,

taking off his reading glasses to contemplate his next move. "What do you think we should do?"

"Well, we certainly can't keep him as sheriff. I think we should appoint a new one before he returns with his corrupt associates."

"Who did you have in mind?" he said, pinching his brow. "I'm not sure we've got anyone qualified to manage such a rowdy group."

Madame paused for a moment, then slowly turned toward Riley.

"I don't suppose..." she said, cocking her head.

"Me?" Riley said, bulging her eyes in disbelief. "But I don't have any experience–"

"You handled another member of their gang easily enough," Madame said. "And you seem to have a passing knowledge of the law."

"But what will I do when he returns with his posse?" Riley said. "I could never stand up to the whole lot of them on my own."

"You can choose more deputies," Madame said. "Plus, Clarence is pretty handy with a shotgun. Once the outlaws see the town is no longer willing to put up with their unlawful ways, hopefully they'll move on to easier pickings."

"I don't know," Riley said. "This is all so sudden–"

"You heard what James said in the gully," Madame said. "He plans to get rid of you one way or the other. Your only choice is to fight or flee."

"Hmm," Riley nodded, realizing how simple it would be for her to run away using her time machine.

But she didn't feel comfortable leaving the rest of the town defenseless against the corrupt sheriff and his hench-men. If she'd learned anything in her brief adventures back in time, it was that if she submitted to bullies, it would only encourage them to terrorize more people.

"Okay," Riley nodded. "I'll do it, at least until we know the town is safe. Where's the best place to find some able-bodied deputies?"

"We can start in the saloon," Madame nodded. "That's where most of the cowboys hang out."

"Let's get started right away then," Riley said, heading toward the door. "The sooner we secure the streets, the better."

"Wait," the mayor said, pulling open his desk drawer. "You're going to need this."

He handed Riley a silver badge with the title Sheriff printed on it, and after Madame helped her pin it to her vest, she smiled at her proudly.

When the two women entered the saloon, everybody turned to squint at the new star on Riley's chest, wondering what had become of James and his posse.

"Listen up," Madame said as a lull fell over the room. "The mayor has appointed a new sheriff and we're looking for deputies. We're offering ten dollars a week to anyone who's interested."

The room fell silent for a moment, then someone shifted his chair noisily, turning toward the pair.

"What happened to the old sheriff and why is he being replaced by a *woman*?" he said, placing extra emphasis on the last word.

"It's come to our attention that James is in cahoots with the bandits," Madame said. "We can no longer trust him to uphold the law. Riley has proven herself capable using a gun, and the mayor has chosen her to step in for the time being."

The men in the room peered at one another for a moment, then they turned back around, resuming their card games and idle chatter.

Riley turned to glance at Madame, shaking her head in confusion.

"Why isn't anybody stepping forward?" she said.

"James made a lot of allies among this group by looking the other way when minor disagreements broke out. Perhaps they were aware of his connection with the Adams gang, and are afraid there will be more trouble."

"I'm not sure this was such a good idea," Riley sighed, wondering what she'd gotten herself into.

Suddenly, a familiar voice emerged from the crowd.

"*I'll* volunteer," she said.

Riley turned toward the bar, noticing Bess walking toward her with a steely grin on her face.

"If none of these cowards will step forward to protect this town, I'll be happy to," she said. "You can't do the job alone, and we've already had experience working together."

"Waiting *tables*," Riley said. "Do you have experience handling a gun?"

"Enough to get by," Bess nodded. "I grew up on a ranch like most of the other locals."

Riley turned toward Madame, shrugging her shoulders.

"What do you think, Madame?" she said. "Can you manage the bar with two less girls?"

"We can repurpose some of the girls from upstairs," she nodded. "The safety of the town is more important than satisfying these limp dicks' prurient desires."

When Riley and Bess entered the sheriff's office, they glanced at the empty jail cell behind the desk and the gun rack lining the wall. Riley pulled open the desk drawer, noticing a chain of keys.

"Keys to the kingdom?" Bess nodded, smiling at Riley.

"This dusty old town is hardly a *kingdom*," Riley chuckled, taking a seat in the sheriff's chair.

"Yes, but at least you're the one in charge," Bess said, peering down at Riley's five-pointed star. "I kind of like the look of you being the new lawman in town."

"I'm not exactly a law*man*..." Riley said.

"Even better," Bess said, pushing Riley's chair back and sitting on her lap while snaking her legs under the armrests. "You're a kick-ass chick with a hot body and a take-no-prisoners attitude."

"I'm not sure the mayor would approve of this kind of behavior on my first day on the job," Riley smiled, grabbing Bess's ass playfully.

"It's pretty quiet right now," Bess said, unbuttoning the top of Riley's shirt. "And those lazy cowboys seem plenty distracted with their card games. It won't hurt for us to take a little break when nobody's looking."

"You're a very bad girl," Riley said, raising Bess's chin to kiss her on the lips. "I might have to make use of that empty cell earlier than planned if you keep behaving like this."

"Oh?" Bess teased. "Do you intend to *cuff* me and teach me a lesson?"

"That's not a bad idea–" Riley said, reaching up to squeeze Bess's breasts.

Suddenly, the front window of their office shattered as a band of horsemen stormed down the center of the main street. Riley threw Bess off her lap and raised out of her chair, peering out the side of the window to see who was creating all the commotion.

"It's the Adams gang," she said, recognizing the leather hat of their ringleader.

She paced over to the gun rack, trying the keys until the cover swung open.

"Do you know how to use a rifle?" she said, pulling one of the Winchesters off the rack.

"Only to shoot *rabbits*," Bess said, peering back at her with a frightened expression.

"Well, these guys are bigger, and a lot slower. It shouldn't be too difficult to pick them off if need be."

She peered around the office, noticing a back door leading to the outhouse.

"Find a location on top of one of the nearby buildings and wait for my signal. If it comes down to it, we may need to act fast."

"What are you planning to do?" Bess said, grasping the barrel of the rifle as Riley handed it to her.

"I'm not sure," Riley said. "I've never been in a situation like this before. But if past experience is any guide, these men will be underestimating our abilities. Just be ready to shoot if things get too hairy."

12

After a few minutes, the band of outlaws returned to the front of the sheriff's office, lining up their horses to block the front exit. Riley peered out the window, seeing a group of five mounted men, with the ringleader in the middle, sneering back at her.

"Come out, little girl," he taunted. "This is no place for a *woman* to hide."

Riley hesitated for a moment, contemplating her next move. She considered ducking out the back, but she knew that would only be shirking her responsibility as the new town sheriff. Somebody would have to stand up to these outlaws, or the town would never be safe. Steeling all of her nerve, she pulled up her britches and opened the front door slowly.

"Well, looky here, boys," the ringleader smiled, seeing the shiny star on her chest. "Looks like we have a new sheriff in town."

"Yes," one of the gang members nodded. "And she's a might prettier than the last one."

"And a whole lot *softer*," the man who'd groped her at the saloon a few days earlier said.

"I'm not as soft as you think," Riley said, spreading her feet a few inches apart in defiance.

"So we've heard," the ringleader said. "I heard you dispatched poor Amos right quick."

"He had what was coming to him," Riley said, glancing up to the rooftops behind the men to see if she could find any sign of Bess.

"I suspect he did," the ringleader nodded. "But there's six of us, and only one of you. Nobody's fast enough to outdraw six guns at the same time."

"Maybe not," Riley growled. "But I'll take the first one who tries."

The ringleader paused for a moment, darting his eyes over Riley's curvy figure. Then his eyes refocused, peering a few feet behind her.

"Not if he's standing *behind* you," he said.

Riley could feel her heart racing, wondering if the ringleader was bluffing, then she heard the floorboards creaking from inside the office. She glanced up, catching some movement on the roof of the general store across the street, noticing Bess kneeling into position and pointing her rifle toward the backs of the gunmen.

"Now then," the ringleader said, seeing that Riley was outnumbered. "There's no need for anyone else to get hurt today. Lay down your arms and go back to your regular job at the saloon, and we'll make sure there's no more trouble."

"Yeah," Charlie grinned, staring at Riley's open blouse. "And we can pick up where we left off."

Riley's eyes darted over the figures of the five outlaws, trying to decide what to do next. She was clearly outgunned, and even if she got off the first shot, she wasn't likely to survive a gun battle surrounded by six armed men. But she realized that if she laid down her gun, it would only give them free license to do whatever they wanted with her and the rest of the girls in Madame's saloon.

When she heard the man cocking his pistol behind her, her eyes suddenly flew open with rage. Dropping to the floorboards of the front porch, she twisted her body, firing two shots into his chest, then she rolled backwards into the entrance as Bess's rifle shot caught the left shoulder of the ringleader. When she slammed the door shut, a fusillade of bullets pounded the front of her office, spraying broken glass all around her.

Realizing she only had seconds before the gang broke through the door, she jumped over the body of the man she'd shot and sprinted through the back exit. Seeing the outhouse as the only building nearby, she rushed into the shelter, latching the door quietly behind her. As she peered through a crack in the siding, she noticed the group of gunmen rushing out the back of the office, peering in both directions to locate the missing girl.

Ugh, she thought, holding her breath against the noxious fumes from the open pit. *What I'd give to be back on the pirate ship, smelling the fresh sea breeze while I poop into the ocean. This probably wasn't the smartest place to hole up against a band of outlaws.*

"You boys spread out in opposite directions to see if you can find the girl," the ringleader said, grimacing as he grasped his shoulder. "I'll look around here to see if she's anywhere nearby."

As the other cowboys disappeared into the alleyways beside the sheriff's office, the ringleader paused, peering toward the closed door of the outhouse.

"You don't really think you can hide from us in the *privy*, do you?" he sneered, walking toward the tiny shed. "Surely that's not where you're going to make your last stand. The outhouse is an ignominious place to meet your end."

As he began firing shots from his pistol and piercing holes in the thin walls, Riley's mind raced, trying to figure a way out of her impossible situation. If the bullets whizzing past her shaking body didn't finish her first, the ringleader would soon kick down the front door and easily pick her off in the enclosed space of the narrow compartment.

Then she remembered one of the scenes from her favorite gangster movie, *The Professional*. In the scene where the hitman and the little girl were cornered in a hotel room, the hitman curled up against the wall above the front door, waiting for their pursuers to enter the room, where he shot them from behind. She jumped up onto the bench and braced her legs against one side of the hut, walking hand-over-hand up toward ceiling, crouching over the entrance as the sideboards creaked from her straining body.

"Come out, come out, wherever you are," the ringleader taunted. "I know you're in there. Why don't we make this easy? Come out with your hands up, and I promise to finish this quickly. You can either go the easy way or the hard way."

Riley grunted, feeling her arm and leg muscles quivering while she struggled to hold her position. She heard the sound of footsteps approaching the entrance, then the ringleader kicked in the door, firing three shots into the empty space.

"What the...?" he muttered, stepping into the enclosure.

He glanced to both sides then he peered up, noticing Riley staring back at him with her pistol aimed squarely at his forehead. He tried to lift his gun, but Riley fired in an instant, and his body slumped back onto the bench, covering the stinking hole.

"That's a fitting resting place for at least *one* of us, asshole," Riley grunted, hopping down and rushing out of the enclosure to evade the remaining gang members, who were circling back to investigate the sound of the shooting.

One of them emerged from the alley beside the sheriff's office, and she drew her pistol, striking him in the stomach. As he crumpled to the ground, she ran past him into the passageway while the rest of the outlaws followed in pursuit. When she emerged onto the main street, she saw Clarence standing on the front steps of the saloon, holding a shotgun.

She dashed in his direction, and when the three remaining men emerged from the alleyway, Bess picked one of them off from above while Clarence dropped another. Realizing there was only one more gunman to contend with, she rushed into an adjacent alley, only to find it blocked from the other side. As she turned around to exit the dead end, she noticed Charlie grinning back at her with his pistol raised to her head.

"It's a shame to have to kill you," he snorted. "I was really looking forward to finishing our business upstairs."

Riley paused for a moment, trying to think of another way out of her predicament.

"Not if the man behind you has anything to do with it," she said.

"You're bluffing," Charlie said.

"Maybe," Riley said. "But are you sure you want to take the chance? If you shoot first, he'll end you before you even have a chance to turn around."

Charlie hesitated for a moment, and when he turned his head partially, she raised her pistol, striking him between the legs.

"You *bitch!*" he shouted, pulling his left hand toward his crotch. "You shot me in the *balls!*"

"You won't be needing them where *you're* going," she said, firing another round into his chest as he tried to lift his shaking gun.

Believing that was the last of the bandits, she walked toward the open end of the alley. Then a familiar figure suddenly stepped into the void, blocking the light.

"That's a pretty impressive performance for your first day on the job," James sneered, walking slowly toward her. "But if I've counted correctly, that's the last of your six shots. You should have taken at least one lesson from Amos. A *real* cowboy carries two pistols on his gun belt, not one."

"It didn't help *him* very much, as I recall," Riley said, drawing her pistol and pulling the trigger to the sound of an empty click.

"It's too bad it has to end this way," James said, walking toward Riley while glancing at her open cleavage. "I might have made you my deputy if things had turned out a little differently."

"I'd *never* be your lackey," Riley hissed, throwing her empty pistol at him.

"Feisty to the end," he smiled, ducking his head and raising his pistol to take aim at Riley. "Any last words?"

Suddenly, Riley heard a loud bang, and James's eyes flung open as his body recoiled, dropping face first onto the sand below her feet.

"Yes," Madame said, holding a smoking shotgun in her hands. "Go *fuck* yourself."

13

Later that night, the whole town feted Riley with a celebration in the saloon. Even the cowboys who'd been reluctant to help her fend off the outlaws seemed relieved to have the corrupt sheriff out of the way. The working girls from upstairs seemed particularly happy with the new gentle treatment they were receiving from their customers. Everybody seemed to realize that with a woman overseeing law and order in Cody, they would be treated differently from now on.

"This looks like a happier lot," Madame said, surveying the room as she clinked whiskey glasses with Riley while they stood chatting next to the bar with Clarence.

"With a lot less *groping*," Riley nodded, watching Bess shuttling drinks to and from the tables.

"After watching how you handled Amos and the rest of the Adams gang, they wouldn't *dare* underestimate your abilities again."

Riley took a gulp of whiskey, placing the empty glass down on the counter.

"Although it's just *me* now having to supervise a bunch of oversexed, drunken cowboys," she said.

"Something tells me things are going to be a lot quieter around here now that the worst of them have been dealt with," Madame said. "But Clarence has still got your back if anybody gets any bright ideas. Isn't that right, Clarence?"

"Absolutely," Clarence said, reaching under the bar to show his shotgun close at hand.

"I appreciate the help earlier today," Riley said, nodding toward the two of them. "I couldn't have managed that gang without both of you stepping in."

"It was the least we could do," Madame said. "Seeing as how you were outnumbered and all."

Bess suddenly returned to the bar to refill her tray, brushing up against Riley as she gave her a wink.

"How's it going out there?" Riley said, rolling her ass softly against Bess's petticoat. "Are the boys behaving themselves for a change?"

"It's amazing how putting on a badge changes everyone's perception of you," Bess nodded. "They know they can't mess with me any longer."

"Do you *miss* wearing that deputy badge?" Riley said, glancing at Bess's upturned breasts in her saloon girl outfit.

"It's a lot safer serving *these* kinds of shots," Bess smiled, peering down at the small glasses Clarence was placing on her tray. "But I do miss our quiet time together in the sheriff's office."

"That didn't last very long," Riley chuckled. "But we should be able to find some alone time after your shift is over. That is, if Madame is agreeable to my taking a break later on tonight also."

"You certainly deserve a rest after your hectic day,"

Madame smiled. "Besides, you no longer work for me. The *mayor* pays your salary now."

"Mmm," Riley said, dropping two pennies on the counter as Clarence refilled her whiskey glass.

She smiled at how cheap everything was a hundred years ago, vowing to pack some modern-day currency with her the next time she traveled back to Boston.

"Don't be silly," Madame said, pushing the coins back along the counter toward her. "Tonight, the drinks are on me."

"Maybe just for one night," Riley smiled. "Unlike the last guy who wore this badge, I intend to honor my obligations."

By two a.m., everything had quieted down in the bar as the last of the cowboys staggered out of the saloon to return home. Riley locked the front door of the sheriff's office then returned to her room on the second floor, finding Bess lying naked on the bed, waiting for her.

"You're not going to sleep on the jail cot in the sheriff's office tonight?" Bess said when Riley closed the door behind her.

"This bed's a lot warmer and more comfortable," Riley smiled, unbuckling her gun belt and hanging it over the back of the chair. "Plus, I could use a little company tonight. I've had enough of that office for one day."

"Yes," Bess said, patting the mattress beside her. "That makes *two* of us. It'll be nice to lay down our arms for once."

Riley pulled off the rest of her clothes then climbed onto the bed, straddling Bess's hips.

"Mmm," she purred, rolling her moist pussy over Bess's

soft bush. "Thanks for helping me out today. That was a close one. I needed every extra gun we could find."

"Sorry I missed with my first shot," Bess said. "After you pulled that fancy trick on the front porch, I had to act fast. Shooting a bunch of outlaws is more difficult than shooting rabbits."

"I'm kind of glad you let me finish off the ringleader," Riley said, pressing her hips down harder over Bess's mound. "It felt kind of good leaving him shitting his pants over the can."

"To the victor go the spoils," Bess nodded, reaching up to squeeze Riley's tits as they began to rock their hips together.

Suddenly Madame stuck her head in the door, grinning at the couple as they made love on the bed.

"Am I interrupting anything?" she said.

"That depends," Riley smiled. "Were you planning on *joining* us, or just standing there and watching?"

"I can't let *you* have all the fun," she said, pulling off her heavy layers of clothes and throwing them over the chair.

"May I?" she said, pausing at the side of the bed, peering down at Bess.

"By all means," Bess smiled.

Madame crawled onto the bed and lifted her knee, straddling Bess's stomach, facing Riley. As the two women began grinding their pussies together, Bess tilted her hips forward, feeling Riley's wet vulva rolling over her throbbing clit. While Madame pressed her sex harder against Bess's mound, Madame and Riley began to kiss, moaning in each other's mouth. Before long, all three women were grunting and rocking their hips in unison, squealing in simultaneous pleasure. After they all came together, Riley and Madame flopped down onto the bed on opposite sides of Bess.

"Now *that's* what I call ride-em-cowboy," Riley panted, smiling at the two women.

"We're going to have to come up with a new unisex term, now that there's a new gunslinger in town," Madame said.

"I dunno," Riley smiled. "Cowperson doesn't have quite the same ring to it."

"What about cowpoke?" Bess said, caressing the two women's breasts.

"I kind of like the sound of gunslinger," Riley said.

"Are you planning to stick around now that you've got a steady job?" Madame said.

"I don't know," Riley said, rolling over to peer at her new friends. "There's an expression where I come from—a rolling stone gathers no moss. I'm a bit of a vagabond."

"Where will you go next?" Bess said.

"I honestly don't know," Riley said. "I just know being a full-time sheriff isn't the life for me."

"We'll be sorry to see you go, wherever it is," Madame said, stroking Riley's bush softly.

"The town is in good hands, now that the troublemakers have been eliminated," Riley nodded.

"The problem is, there's always a new band of trouble-makers to take their place," Madame frowned.

"Mmm," Riley nodded, resting her head on Bess's shoulder as she drifted off to sleep.

When she awoke a few hours later, she got up and raised her hand to the top of the valence to retrieve her time machine, slipping it into her back pocket as she quietly got dressed. Madame stirred for a moment, peering in her direction.

"Where are you going?" she said, wondering why Riley was putting on her sheriff uniform in the middle of the night.

"I have to use the privy," she lied.

"You only need a chemise at this time of night," Madame said. "Nobody will notice you sneaking out the back."

"I'm not taking any chances with all these randy cowboys roaming about," Riley said, deciding it would be better to travel through time fully dressed this time.

"Okay," Madame said, resting her head back down beside Bess.

Riley tiptoed down the stairs then untied her horse from the hitching post in front of the saloon, trotting her horse slowly down the main street. When she reached the outskirts of town, she dismounted and slapped the animal's behind, sending it back in the direction of Cody.

Then she pulled her time travel device from her back pocket, tapping the screen. The familiar funnel began to swirl over the glass, and as it began to rise up in a three-dimensional vortex, she peered back at the saloon in the distance, noticing a dim light in Bess's room, with the curtains pulled to the side. As she lifted her hand to say goodbye to her friends, she felt herself pulled into the funnel, tumbling through the portal again, unsure where she would land.

When she fell into the middle of a pitch-black field, she looked up, noticing loud explosions overhead. As she kneeled in the grass trying to get her bearings, an enormous steel tank rolled past her with a swastika emblazoned on the side.

Jesus, she muttered to herself. *Why do I always have to end up in the middle of a conflict?*

Suddenly, a G.I. wearing a U.S. army helmet pulled up beside her, dragging her back down into the grass.

"What in God's name are you doing in the middle of no-man's-land?" the rugged soldier said. "And what are you doing wearing a cowboy hat and a Colt 45?"

"It's complicated," Riley sighed, realizing she'd gotten herself into a whole heap of new trouble...

R*eady for more steamy chills and thrills? Order the next exciting volume in Riley's Time Travel Adventures:*

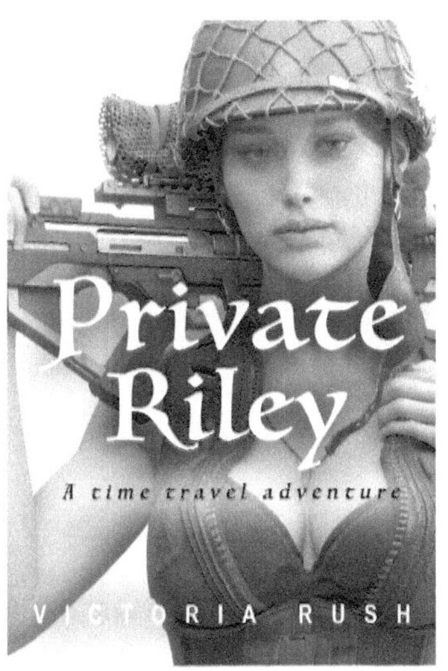

Sometimes it takes a woman to disarm the most powerful men...

FOLLOW VICTORIA RUSH:

Want to keep informed of my latest erotic book releases? Sign up for my newsletter and receive a FREE bonus book:

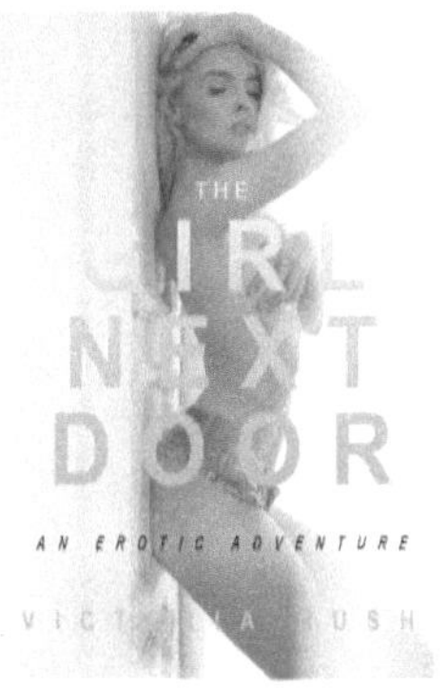

Spying on the neighbors just got a lot more interesting...